Let's Pretend

Tony Bradman

Illustrated by Lesley Harker

CAMBRIDGE
UNIVERSITY PRESS

I'm a pirate on the sea,

I'm a singer on TV.

I'm an astronaut in Space,

I'm a runner in a race.

I'm a giant with big feet,

I'm a ghost in a sheet.

I'm a teacher in a school,

I'm a swimmer in a pool.

I'm a dancer dressed in red,

I'm so tired . . .

. . . I'm off to bed!